To Sriram, Rasika, and Pritam, who are my story —M.S.

To Maragadam (sorry I accidentally used to call you
Magaradam), who meticulously designed intricate
mehndi on our palms one unforgettable
summer in Coimbatore —S.P.

THIS IS A BORZOI BOOK PUBLISHED BY ALFRED A. KNOPF

Text copyright © 2023 by Meera Sriram
Jacket art and interior illustrations copyright © 2023 by Sandhya Prabhat

All rights reserved. Published in the United States by Alfred A. Knopf, an imprint of
Random House Children's Books, a division of Penguin Random House LLC, New York.

Knopf, Borzoi Books, and the colophon are registered trademarks of Penguin Random House LLC.

Visit us on the Web! rhcbooks.com

Educators and librarians, for a variety of teaching tools, visit us at RHTeachersLibrarians.com

Library of Congress Cataloging-in-Publication Data is available upon request.
ISBN 978-0-593-42710-1 (trade) – ISBN 978-0-593-42711-8 (lib. bdg.) –
ISBN 978-0-593-42712-5 (ebook)

The text of this book is set in 14-point Givens Antiqua.
The illustrations were created digitally.
Book design by Nicole Gastonguay

MANUFACTURED IN CHINA
10 9 8 7 6 5 4 3 2 1

First Edition

A GARDEN in my HANDS

Written by **Meera Sriram**   Illustrated by **Sandhya Prabhat**

Alfred A. Knopf   New York

Stories and seeds
Mama plants in my palm
for a wedding tomorrow.
We'll go with Dada and Dadi!

Falling raindrops,
drizzle on buds—
Mama sings me
her monsoon memory.

She smiles and shares
her wedding story
of pearls on a string,
petals on a vine.

Teardrops. Crisscrosses.
Mama adds thorns to roses—
she tells me
of ancestors long gone.

My henna still fresh
like damp earth.
I'll keep it warm all night
for the deepest red.

Careful not to snip
or smudge a story.

My hands like a scarecrow . . .
Oh no! I smear a lush spot.

Mama lends a hand—
and I stain her new scarf.
My two sorry arms
wilt with worry.

I search for a home
for my half-dry hands.
I tuck my henna in
and snuggle with our stories.

In soft paper layers
and old cotton gloves,
I hug the wide world
and drift into a dream.

When my eyes catch the sun,
I hold my breath.
What if it's a mess?
What if I lose a story?

As I rub off dry flakes,
a sigh leaves my chest.

I wash away my worries.

I float into a garden.
A bouquet of flowers,
peacocks, and paisleys—
beautiful stories,
in the most perfect shade!

My fairy-tale hands
match my lehenga.

Mama leans over,
kisses my garden.

Dada peers into my palm.
Dadi traces every swirl.
Our hands like a garland,

we sway to the beat.

The sweet smell of henna,
and stories we carry,
fill us with pride
of a faraway home.

A garden in my hands,
I will tend for days.
A garden in my heart,
I will hold forever.

Where did henna come from?

Henna is made from the crushed leaves of the henna plant. The word *henna* comes from Arabic. The word *mehndi,* referring to the henna paste, is commonly used in India and is derived from Sanskrit.

    Henna has been around for many centuries and was used by several early civilizations. Ancient Egyptians colored the hair, fingers, and toes of pharaohs before mummification. It is also believed that applying henna on the body might have originated in the deserts of South Asia and the Middle East, where people "wore" henna on their hands and feet for its cooling effect.

    While henna is mostly used to create body art, it is also a natural dye for hair and cloth and is popular in herbal medicine.

When do we use henna?

Henna is used as a sign of celebration for religious holidays, festivals, and weddings. In several cultures around the world, it is common for a bride (and sometimes a groom) to apply elaborate henna designs before the wedding. In some places, it is also used to ward off evil.

How does henna stain our skin, hair, and nails?

The henna plant contains a pigment called lawsone. Crushing or grinding the leaves releases the lawsone molecules. When we apply henna to our skin, hair, or nails, the lawsone molecules attach to their outer layers. Later they interact with keratin, a protein our body produces, and air, leaving a stain that is red orange in color.

What are some popular designs?

Traditional henna designs vary across cultures. Elaborate floral designs are common in South Asia and in Islamic cultures. Simple motifs include paisley, flower, or leaf. Traditional designs also include peacocks and animal faces. Sometimes they feature script lettering or religious symbols. In Africa, bold, geometric patterns are very common.

How do we apply henna?

1. The bright green henna powder is mixed with water to make a thick, greenish-brown paste. Sometimes a little lemon juice is added.
2. The paste is poured into a small plastic cone (similar to frosting for cake decorating). Ready-made cones full of henna are also available.
3. The cone is squeezed carefully to draw designs, a skill that can be mastered with practice. Henna can be applied anywhere on the body. However, the final color of the design will appear brighter on palms and the soles of feet. Henna is also commonly applied on the back of hands, up to the wrist or elbow, and on feet up to the ankle.
4. After the designs are drawn, the decorated areas are left untouched for several hours. The longer the henna stays, the darker its color!
5. After dried henna is washed off, the beautiful designs and patterns appear in a bright shade of red and stay on for a few weeks.

Here are a few typical henna designs to draw. Try them first with a pencil on paper!

Author's Note

When I was a kid growing up in India, my mother often ground henna leaves and applied henna paste to my palms and fingers. I would walk around all evening with my arms stretched out in front or to the side, careful not to mess up any part of the design. When I also had my feet done, which was rare, I would walk around on my heels. I even saved old shirts and skirts just for henna nights so my good clothes wouldn't get stained.

I remember the cool feeling on my freshly done hands while the air around me was hot and sticky. At night, my mother would feed me my dinner and prepare my special bed, usually a straw mat on the warm open terrace. In the morning, I would quickly rub off the dry flakes and rush to the sink, eager to see the shade of red. I still love henna, and every time I smell my hennaed palm, it takes me back home—to my mother, quiet summer nights, and many childhood joys.